Molly and the Lighthouse published by Graffeg in 2020.
Copyright © Graffeg Limited 2020.

Text copyright © Malachy Doyle, illustrations copyright
© Andrew Whitson, design and production Graffeg Limited.
This publication and content is protected by copyright © 2020.

Malachy Doyle and Andrew Whitson are hereby identified
as the authors of this work in accordance with section 77
of the Copyrights, Designs and Patents Act 1988.

A CIP Catalogue record for this book is available from
the British Library.

Molly and the Lighthouse ISBN 9781913134914
Mali a'r Goleudy (Welsh edition) ISBN 9781913634179
Muireann agus an Teach Solais (Irish edition) ISBN 9781912929061

Molly and the Lighthouse eBook ISBN 9781913634643
Mali a'r Goleudy eBook ISBN 9781913634636
Muireann agus an Teach Solais eBook ISBN 9781913634650

1 2 3 4 5 6 7 8 9

For Megan – M. D.
For Eithne and Orla – A. W.

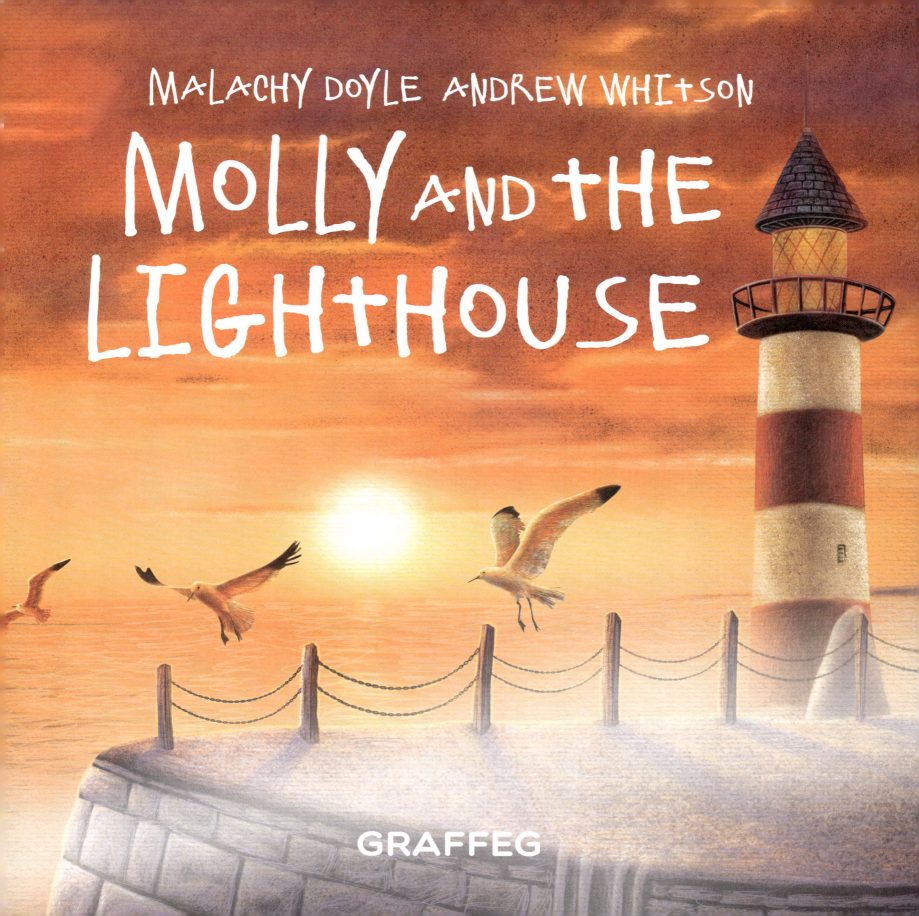

The lighthouse was one of Molly's very favourite things on the whole island.

All night long the brightness of its beam kept her company, going round and around, whatever the weather.

'One, two, three...' Molly counted, and by the time she got to seventeen – somehow it was always seventeen – there it was again, lighting up the room.

And lighting up the shelf where her little doll, Megan, slept.

3

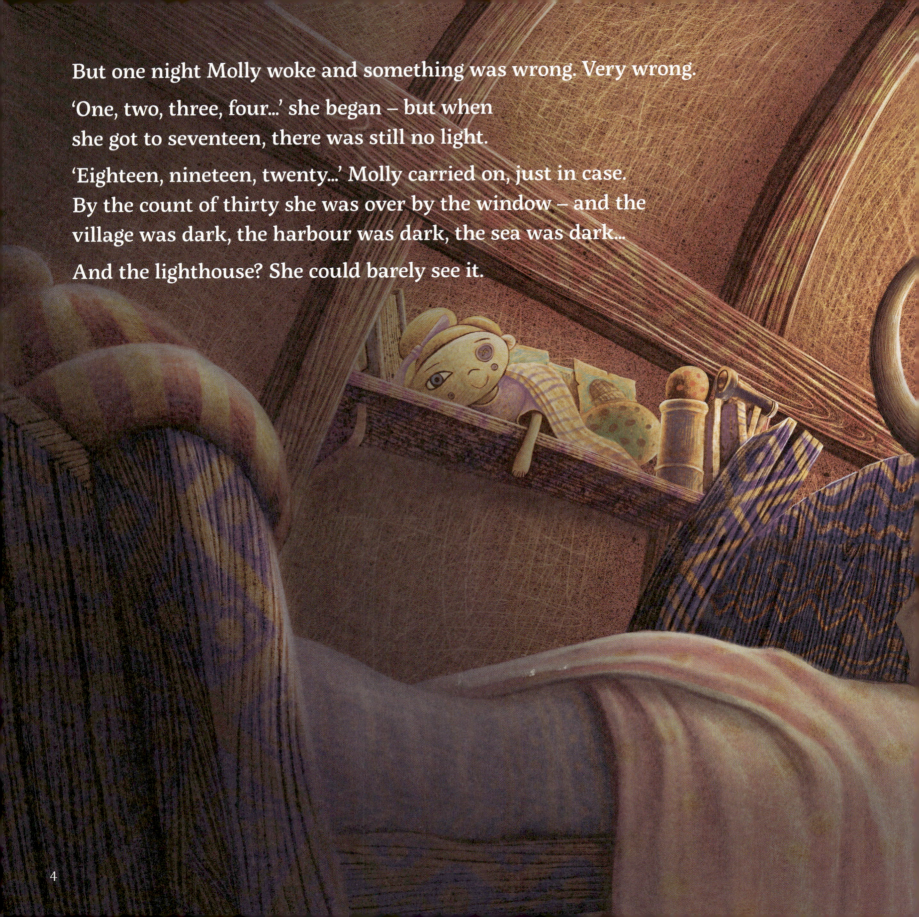

But one night Molly woke and something was wrong. Very wrong.

'One, two, three, four...' she began – but when
she got to seventeen, there was still no light.

'Eighteen, nineteen, twenty...' Molly carried on, just in case.
By the count of thirty she was over by the window – and the
village was dark, the harbour was dark, the sea was dark...

And the lighthouse? She could barely see it.

'Dylan! Wake up!' cried Molly - for her best friend was staying over, while his mother was off the island. 'The lighthouse isn't flashing!'

Then, 'Look!' she said, pointing. For out there, on the darkened sea, Molly had spotted one tiny light. The light of their fathers' little red fishing-boat.

'They won't be able to tell where the sharp rocks are!' gasped Dylan. 'Our dads won't be able to find a safe way back into harbour!'

7

'Wait here, children,' said Molly's mum, when they woke her and told her. 'I'll go down to the harbour wall and make a fire, to guide them back in.'

'Yes, but what about Old Jamesie?' asked Molly, who was fond of the lighthouse keeper. 'He'd never let the light go out. There must be something wrong!'

'You're right,' said her mum. 'Someone needs to check he's OK.'

'We'll go, won't we, Dylan?' said Molly.

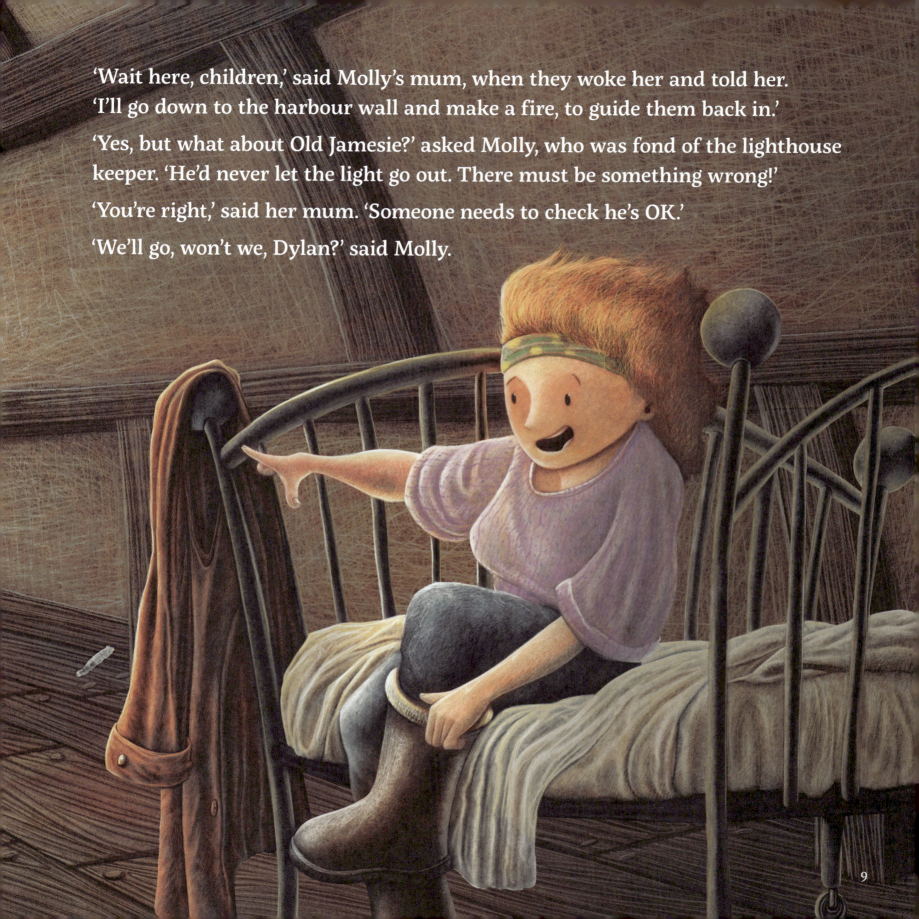

She grabbed Megan, her little doll, and down the
wooden steps they ran, till they came to the rickety
walkway that led to the lighthouse.

'You'll be OK, Dylan,' said Molly. 'Just follow me.'

The sea splashed up and over their boots, but they
kept on going. They had to!

'Ten... twenty... thirty... forty...' Molly counted, as they climbed the narrow steps, round and around to the very top of the lighthouse.

At last they reached the control room. But the massive light – that should have been shining on the whole world all around – was dark, completely dark.

There was no sign of her mother's fire, down on the harbour wall, and all Molly could make out on the cold sea below was a pin-prick of light from their fathers' boat. But where was it now? Was it closer to the rocks?

Molly knew that she and Dylan had to get the beam of the lighthouse back on, and quickly. But how?

'Look, Molly!'
cried Dylan.

16

'Over here!' came a faint cry.

It was Old Jamesie, collapsed on the floor.

'What happened?' cried Dylan, hurrying over.

'Never mind me, boy – pull the lever!' wheezed
the keeper.

'Yes but which one?' said Molly.
'There's loads of them!'

But Old Jamesie had fallen silent.

And then she spotted it, high above her –
a big red heavy-duty one...

'That's it!' cried Molly, pulling a chair over.
'It must be!'

She put a stool on the chair – but it still wasn't high enough.

'We're running out of time, Dylan! Pass Megan up!'

Molly flung the little doll at the lever.

Megan somehow wrapped her floppy arms around it.

Molly tugged and tugged her, but the switch wouldn't budge.

'We need to pull harder! ' cried Dylan, grabbing hold of
Molly's boots.

So Dylan pulled Molly, Molly pulled Megan,
Megan pulled the lever and...

CRASH!

Everyone hit the floor with a mighty THUD!

Molly saw a blinding flash as the magnificent light above them came back on, flooding the world, inside and out, with brightness.

And then her eyes closed.

24

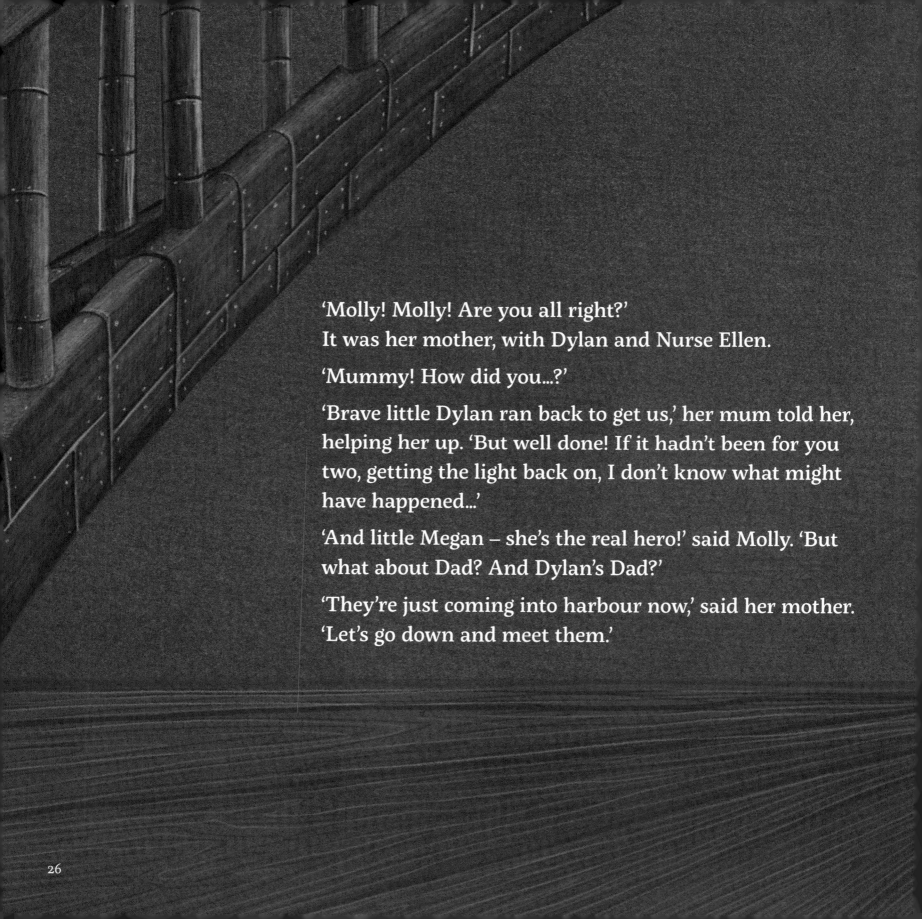

'Molly! Molly! Are you all right?'
It was her mother, with Dylan and Nurse Ellen.

'Mummy! How did you...?'

'Brave little Dylan ran back to get us,' her mum told her, helping her up. 'But well done! If it hadn't been for you two, getting the light back on, I don't know what might have happened...'

'And little Megan – she's the real hero!' said Molly. 'But what about Dad? And Dylan's Dad?'

'They're just coming into harbour now,' said her mother. 'Let's go down and meet them.'

'What about Old Jamesie?' asked Molly, as they started back down the spiral staircase. 'Is he OK?'

'I must have passed out for a bit,' wheezed the lighthouse keeper, from above. 'But I'll be fine.'

'You need to rest, Jamesie,' they heard Nurse Ellen telling him. 'No more steps for a few weeks, I'd say.'

'Three hundred and forty seven...' muttered Molly. 'Steps,' she added, with a smile.

'You and your counting, girl!' said her mum, laughing.

The harbour, when they got there, was lit by the warm glow of the fire that Molly's mother and the other villagers had built.

And there was the little red fishing boat – with all three fathers of the island on board – chugging into port, safe and well.

'Dad!' cried Dylan.

'My Daddy!' yelled Molly.

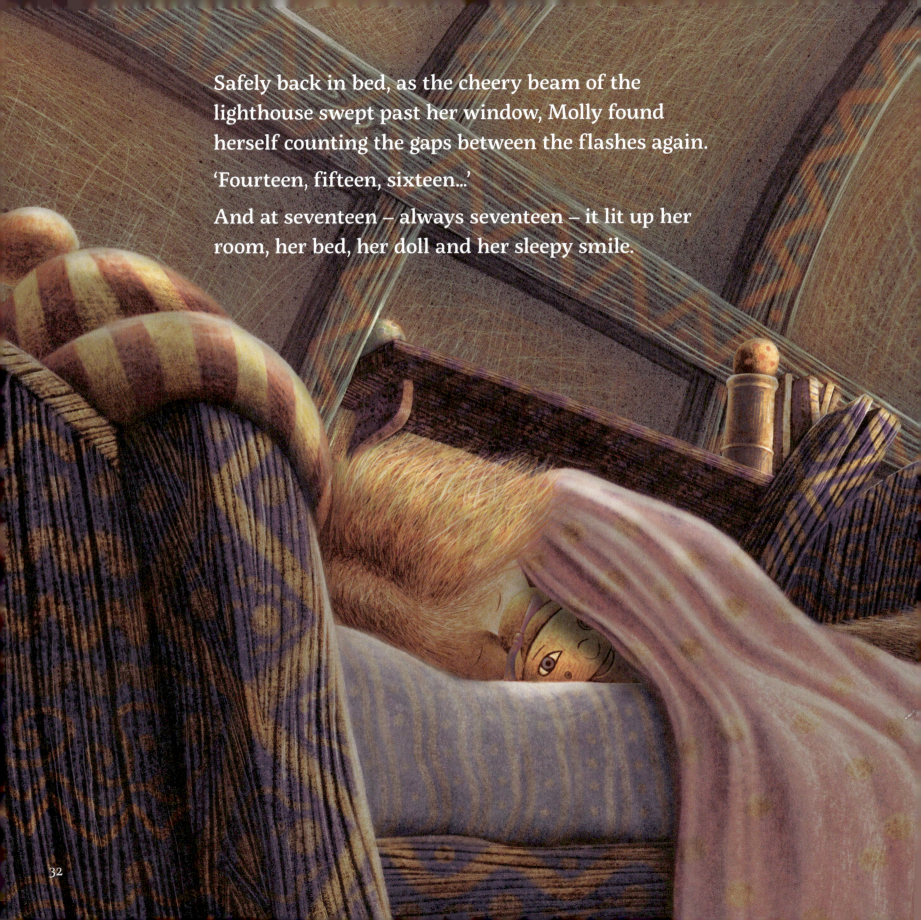

Safely back in bed, as the cheery beam of the lighthouse swept past her window, Molly found herself counting the gaps between the flashes again.

'Fourteen, fifteen, sixteen...'

And at seventeen – always seventeen – it lit up her room, her bed, her doll and her sleepy smile.

33

Malachy Doyle

Malachy Doyle grew up by the sea in Northern Ireland, and after living in Wales for many years has returned to Ireland. He and his wife Liz bought an old farmhouse on a small island off the coast of Donegal, where they live with their dogs, cats and ducks.

Malachy has had well over a hundred books published, from pop-up books for toddlers to gritty teenage novels. Over the years he has won many prestigious book awards, and his work is available in around thirty languages.

As well as the two previous stories in the Molly series, *Molly and the Stormy Sea* and *Molly and the Whale*, his recent books include *The Miracle of Hanukkah*, *Rama and Sita*, *Jack and the Jungle* and *Big Bad Biteasaurus* (Bloomsbury), *Fug and the Thumps* (Firefly Press), *Cinderfella* (Walker Books) and *Ootch Cootch* (Graffeg), which is illustrated by his daughter, Hannah Doyle.

Andrew Whitson

Andrew Whitson is an award-winning artist and Belfast native who likes to be called Mr. Ando! He lives in an old house which is nestled discreetly on the side of a misty hill; at the edge of a magic wood, below an enchanted castle in the shadow of a giant's nose. His house looks down over Belfast Harbour where the Titanic was built and up at the Belfast Cavehill where an American B-17 Flying Fortress bomber plane once crashed during World War II!

Mr. Ando makes pictures for books in the tower of a very old church and works so late that he often gets locked in. He has therefore forged a secret magic key which he keeps at his side at all times and uses to escape from the church when there is no one else around.

Mr. Ando has illustrated over twenty books under his own name, the most recent of which being the *Molly* series with Malachy Doyle and the award winning *Rita* series of picture books with Myra Zepf.